SPIDERWICK CHRONICLES

GOBLINS ATTACK
SPECIAL EDITION OF THE SEEING STONE

VOLUME ONE
with EXCLUSIVE LOST CHAPTER

Tony DiTerlizzi *and* Holly Black

Simon and Schuster Books for Young Readers
New York   London   Toronto   Sydney

SIMON AND SCHUSTER UK LTD
Africa House, 64-78 Kingsway, London WC2B 6AH
A CBS Company

Originally published in the USA by Simon & Schuster
Books for Young Readers, an imprint of
Simon & Schuster Children's Division, New York.

This edition published exclusively for
Nestlé breakfast cereals 2007

The text type for this book is set in Cochin.
The display types are set in Nevins Hand and Rackham.
The illustrations are rendered in pen and ink.

The rights of Tony DiTerlizzi and Holly Black to be
identified as authors of this work has been asserted
in accordance with sections 77 and 78 of the Copyright,
Designs and Patents Act, 1988.

A CIP catalogue record for this book is available from the
· British Library

ISBN-10: 1-84738-157-X
ISBN-13: 978-1-84738-157-6

Printed and bound in Great Britain by
Clays Ltd, St Ives plc

Table of Contents

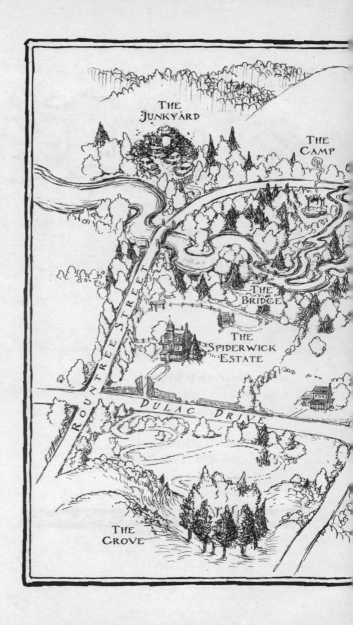

THE
JUNKYARD

THE
CAMP

THE
BRIDGE

THE
SPIDERWICK
ESTATE

ROUNTREE STREET

DULAC DRIVE

THE
GROVE

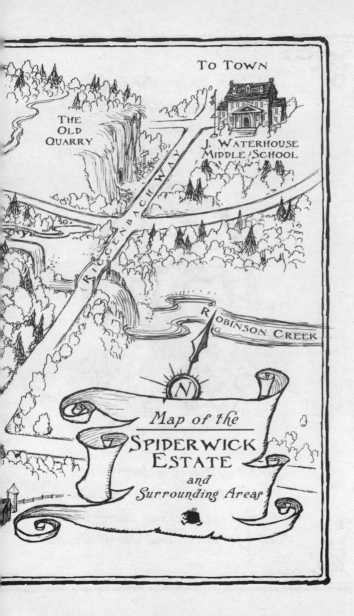

TO TOWN

THE OLD QUARRY

J. WATERHOUSE MIDDLE SCHOOL

RIGGENBACH WAY

ROBINSON CREEK

N

Map of the
SPIDERWICK
ESTATE
and
Surrounding Areas

Welcome to our daring tale,
but there's a little twist:
This book is not the very start.
That's right. There's stuff you missed!

THE GRACE KIDS

So let us take you back in time,
back to our starting place,
where you can meet our heroes three—
Mallory, Simon, and Jared Grace.

They'd left the city far behind
and moved out to the sticks,
to a musty, dusty old estate
with the name of SPIDERWICK.

A. SPIDERWICK

And no sooner had they settled in
than mysteries arose.
A secret room! A long-lost book!
A houseguest filled with woes!

And, oh, the woe this creature caused!
And, oh, the grief and shame,
for every prank this rascal pulled,
poor Jared got the blame.

THE
BOCCART

But that lost book was filled with clues.
When found, it set things right.
And in that secret room a brownie
stepped into the light.

He cautioned our young heroes three
of troubles deep and drastic
if they kept the book, Spiderwick's guide
to worlds close and fantastic.

THIMBLETACK

That brings you up to speed, dear friend,
and now you have to choose:
Turn the page or close the book?
What have you to lose?

The place looked as bad as Jared felt.

Chapter One

IN WHICH More Than a Cat Goes Missing

The late bus dropped Jared Grace at the bottom of his street. From there it was an uphill climb to the dilapidated old house where his family was staying until his mother found something better or his crazy old aunt wanted it back. The red and gold leaves of the low-hanging trees around the gate made the gray shingles look forlorn. The place looked as bad as Jared felt.

He couldn't believe he'd had to stay after school already.

It wasn't like he didn't try to get along with

the other kids. He just wasn't good at it. Take today, for example. Sure, he'd been drawing a brownie while the teacher was talking, but he was still paying attention. More or less. And she didn't have to hold up his drawing in front of the whole class. After that, the kids wouldn't stop bothering him. Before he knew it, he was ripping some boy's notebook in half.

He'd hoped things would be *better* at this school. But since his parents' divorce, things had gone from bad to worse.

Jared walked into the kitchen. His twin, Simon, sat at the old farmhouse table with an untouched saucer of milk in front of him.

Simon looked up. "Have you seen Tibbs?"

"I just got home." Jared went to the fridge and took a swig of apple juice. It was so cold that it made his head hurt.

"Well, did you see him *outside*?" Simon

asked. "I've looked everywhere."

Jared shook his head. He didn't care about the stupid cat. She was just the newest member of Simon's menagerie. One more animal wanting to be petted or fed, or jumping on his lap when he was busy.

Jared didn't know why he and Simon were so different. In movies, identical twins got cool powers like reading each other's minds with a look. It figured that the most real-life twins could do was wear the same-size pants.

Their sister, Mallory, thundered down the stairs, lugging a large bag. The hilts of fencing swords stuck out from one end.

"Hey, good job getting detention, nutcase." Mallory slung the bag over her shoulder and walked toward the back door. "At least this time, no one's nose got broken."

"Don't tell Mom, okay, Mal?" Jared pleaded.

"Whatever. She's going to find out sooner or later." Mallory shrugged and headed out onto the lawn. Clearly this new fencing team was even more competitive than the last. Mallory had taken to practicing at every spare moment. It bordered on obsessive.

"Hey, good job getting detention, nutcase."

"I'm going to Arthur's library," Jared said, and started up the stairs.

"But you have to help me find Tibbs. I waited for you to get home so you could help."

"I don't *have* to do anything." Jared took the stairs two at a time.

In the upstairs hall he opened the linen closet and went inside. Behind the stacks of mothball-packed, yellowed sheets was the door to the house's secret room.

It was dim, lit faintly by a single window, and had the musty smell of old dust. The walls were lined with crumbling books. A massive desk covered in old papers and glass jars dominated one side of the room. Great-Great-Uncle Arthur's secret library. Jared's favorite place.

He glanced back at the painting that hung next to the entrance. A portrait of Arthur Spiderwick peered down at him with small eyes

half hidden behind tiny, round glasses. Arthur
didn't look that old, but he had a pinched mouth
and he seemed stuffy. He certainly didn't seem
like someone who would believe in faeries.

Opening the first drawer on the left-hand side of the desk, Jared tugged free a cloth-wrapped book: *Arthur Spiderwick's Field Guide to the Fantastical World Around You.* He'd only found it a few weeks before, but already Jared had come to think of it as *his*. He kept it with him most of the time, sometimes even sleeping with it under his pillow. He would have even brought it to school, but he was afraid someone would take it from him.

There was a faint sound inside the wall.

"Thimbletack?" Jared called softly.

He could never be sure when the house brownie was around.

Jared put the book down next to his latest project—a portrait of his dad. No one, not even Simon, knew that Jared had been practicing drawing. He wasn't very good—in fact, he was awful. But the Guide was for recording stuff, and to record well, he was going to have to learn to draw. Still, after today's humiliation, he didn't feel much like bothering. To be honest, he felt like tearing the picture of his father to pieces.

"There is a fell smell in the air," said a voice close to Jared's ear. "Best take care."

He whirled around to see a small nut-brown man dressed in a doll-size shirt and pants made from a dress sock. He was standing on one of the bookshelves at Jared's eye level, holding on to a piece of thread. At the top of the shelf, Jared could see the glint of a silver needle that the brownie had used to rappel down with.

"Thimbletack," Jared said, "what's wrong?"

"Could be trouble, could be nought. Whatever it is, it's what you wrought."

"What?"

19

"You kept the book despite my advice. Sooner or later there'll be a price."

"You always say that," said Jared. "What about the price for the sock you cut up to make your outfit? Don't tell me that was Aunt Lucinda's."

Thimbletack's eyes flashed. "Do not laugh, not today. You will learn to fear the fey."

Jared sighed and walked to the window. The last thing he needed was more trouble. Below, he could see the whole backyard. Mallory was close to the carriage house, stabbing at the air with her foil. Further out, near the broken-down plank fence that separated the yard from the nearby forest, Simon stood, hands cupped, probably calling for that stupid cat. Beyond that, thick trees obscured Jared's view. Downhill, in the distance, a highway cut through the woods, looking like a black snake in tall grass.

Thimbletack grabbed hold of the thread and swung over to the window ledge. He started to speak, then just stared outside. Finally he seemed to get his voice back. "Goblins in the wood. Doesn't look good. My warning comes too late. There's no help for your fate."

"Where?"

"By the fence. Have you no sense?"

Jared squinted and looked in the direction the brownie indicated. There was Simon, standing very still and staring at the grass in an odd

21

way. Jared watched in horror as his brother started to struggle. Simon twisted and struck out, but there was nothing there.

"Simon!" Jared tried to force the window open, but it was nailed shut. He pounded on the glass.

Then Simon fell to the ground, still fighting some invisible foe. A moment later, he disappeared.

"I don't see anything!" he shouted at Thimbletack. "What is going on?"

Thimbletack's black eyes gleamed. "I had forgotten, your eyes are rotten. But there is a way, if you do what I say."

"You're talking about the Sight, aren't you?"

The brownie nodded.

"But how come I can see you and not the goblins?"

"We can choose to show what we want you to know."

Jared grabbed the Guide and ruffled through pages he knew nearly by heart: sketches, watercolor illustrations, and notes in his uncle's scratchy handwriting.

"Here," Jared said.

The little brownie leapt from the ledge to the desk.

The page beneath Jared's fingers showed different ways to get the Sight. He scanned quickly. "'Red hair. Being the seventh son of a seventh son. Faerie bathwater'?" He stopped at the last and looked up at Thimbletack, but the little brownie was pointing excitedly down the page. The illustration showed it clearly, a stone with a hole through the middle, like a ring.

"With the lens of stone, you can see what's

The little brownie was pointing excitedly.

not shown." With that, Thimbletack jumped from the desk. He skittered across the floor toward the door to the linen closet.

"We don't have time to look for rocks," Jared yelled, but what could he do except follow?

It smelled of gasoline and mildew.

Chapter Two

IN WHICH Several Things Are Taken, Including a Test

Thimbletack sprinted across the lawn, hopping from shadow to shadow. Mallory was still fencing against the wall of the old carriage house, her back to where Simon had been.

Jared walked up behind her and tugged the headphones off her ears by the cord.

She turned, foil pointing at his chest. "What?"

"Simon's been grabbed by goblins!"

Mallory's eyes narrowed. She looked around the lawn. "Goblins?"

"Must make haste." Thimbletack's voice was as shrill as a bird's. "No time to waste."

"Come on." Jared gestured toward the carriage house where the little brownie was waiting. "Before they get us."

"SIMON!" Mallory shouted.

"Shut up." Jared took her arm and yanked her into the carriage house, closing the door after them. "They're going to hear you."

"Who is going to hear me?" Mallory demanded. *"Goblins?"*

Jared ignored her.

Neither one of them had been inside the building before. It smelled of gasoline and mildew. A tarp covered an old black car. Shelves lined the walls, cluttered with metal tins and mason jars half-filled with brown and yellow liquids. There were even stalls where horses must have been stabled long ago. A stack of boxes and leather trunks occupied one corner.

Thimbletack hopped up on a can of paint and pointed toward the boxes. "Hurry! Hurry! If they come, we must scurry!"

"If Simon got grabbed by goblins, why are we rooting through garbage?" Mallory asked.

"Here," Jared said, holding out the book and pointing to the picture of the stone. "We're looking for *this*."

"Oh, great," she said. "It'll be so easy to find in this mess."

"Just hurry," said Jared.

The first trunk contained a saddle, a few bridles, some combs, and other equipment for taking care of horses. Simon would have been fascinated. Jared and Mallory opened the next box together. It was full of old, rusted tools. Then they found a few boxes stuffed with tableware wrapped in dirty towels.

"Aunt Lucinda must have never thrown out anything," Jared said.

"Here's another one." Mallory sighed as she dragged a small wooden crate over to her brother. The top slid open in a dusty groove, revealing wadded up newspapers.

"Look how old these are," Mallory said. "This one says 1910."

"I didn't even think there were newspapers in 1910," said Jared.

Inside each crumpled piece of paper was a different item. Jared unrolled one to discover a pair of metal binoculars. In another he found a magnifying glass. The print below it was made huge. "This one's from 1927. They're all different."

Jared picked up another page.

"Hey, look at this." Mallory straightened one of the sheets. "1885. 'Local boy lost.' Says he was eaten by a bear. Look at the surviving brother's name! 'Arthur Spiderwick.'"

"There it is! This is his!" Thimbletack said, climbing into the box. When he resurfaced, he held the strangest eyepiece Jared had ever seen.

It covered only a single eye and attached to the face with an adjustable

The strangest eyepiece

nose clip as well as two leather straps and a chain. Backed in stiff, brown leather, four metal clamps waited to hold a lens of some kind. But the strangest thing about the device was the series of magnifying lenses on movable metal arms.

Thimbletack let Jared take the eyepiece and turn it over in his hands. Then he took a smooth stone with a hole through the center from behind his back.

"The lens of stone." Jared reached for it.

Thimbletack stepped back. "Here you must prove yourself or get nothing from this elf."

Jared stared in horror. "We don't have time for games."

"Time or not, you must tell if you will use this stone well."

"I only need it to find Simon," Jared said. "I'll give it right back."

Thimbletack cocked an eyebrow.

Jared tried again. "I promise that I won't let anyone use it—except Mallory—and, well, Simon. Come on! You're the one that suggested the stone in the first place."

"A human boy is like a snake. His promises are easy to break."

Jared's eyes narrowed. He could feel the frustration and anger rising up in him. His hands curled into fists. "Give me the stone."

Thimbletack said nothing.

"Give it to me."

"Jared?" Mallory cautioned.

But Jared barely heard her. There was a roaring in his ears as he reached out and grabbed hold of Thimbletack. The little brownie squirmed in his grasp, abruptly changing shape into a lizard, a rat that bit Jared's hand, then a slippery eel that flailed wetly. Jared was bigger, though, and he held fast. Finally, the stone dropped free, hitting the floor with a clatter. Jared covered it with his foot before he let

Thimbletack go. The brownie disappeared as Jared picked up the stone.

"Maybe you shouldn't have done that," said Mallory.

"I don't care." Jared put his bitten finger in his mouth. "We have to find Simon."

"Does that thing work?" Mallory asked.

"Let's see." Jared held the stone up to his eye and looked out the window.

"They're headed right for us."

Chapter Three

IN WHICH Mallory Finally Gets to Put Her Rapier to Good Use

Through the small hole in the stone, Jared saw goblins. There were five of them, all with faces like frogs' and eyes that were dead white with no pupil at all. Hairless, cat-like ears stuck up from their heads, and their teeth were pieces of shattered glass and small, jagged rocks. Their green, bloated bodies moved swiftly over the lawn. One held a stained sack while the rest scented the air like dogs, moving in the direction of the carriage house. Jared backed away from the window, almost tripping on an old bucket.

"They're headed right for us," he whispered, ducking down.

Mallory gripped her foil more tightly, knuckles white. "What about Simon?"

"I didn't see him."

She lifted up her head and peered outside. "I don't see *anything*," she said.

Jared crouched down with the stone clutched in his palm. He could hear the goblins outside, grunting and shuffling as they got closer. He didn't dare look through the stone again.

Then Jared heard the sound of old wood snapping.

A rock hit one of the windows.

"They're coming," Jared said. He shoved the Guide into his backpack, not bothering to buckle it.

"Coming?" Mallory replied. "I think they're here."

Claws scraped at the side of the barn and little barks came from beneath the window. Jared's stomach turned to lead. He couldn't move.

"We have to do something," he whispered.

"We're going to have to make a run for the house," Mallory whispered back.

"We can't," Jared said. The memory of the goblins' jagged teeth and claws wouldn't leave him.

"A couple more planks and they'll be inside."

He nodded numbly, steeling himself to rise. Fumbling, he tried to fit the stone into the eye-piece and attach it to his head. The clip pinched his nose.

"On my mark," said Mallory. "One. Two. Three. Go!"

She opened the door and they both sprinted toward the house. Goblins hurtled after them. Clawed hands caught at Jared's clothes. He wrenched free and ran on.

Mallory was faster. She was almost to the door of the house when a goblin caught the back of Jared's shirt and pulled hard. He went down on his stomach in the grass. The stone flew out of the monocle. He dug his fingers into the dirt, holding on as much as he could, but he was being dragged backward.

He could feel the clasps on his pack loosening, and he screamed.

Mallory turned. Instead of running on toward the house, she started running back to him. Her fencing sword was still in her hand, but there was no way she could know what she was up against.

GOBLIN

He was being dragged backward.

"Mallory!" Jared shouted. "No! Run away!"

At least one goblin must have gone past him, because he saw Mallory's arm jerk and heard her cry out. The headphones were ripped free from her neck. She spun and lashed out with the rapier, dealing a stinging blow to the air. It didn't seem like she had hit anything. She swung the sword in an arc, but again, nothing.

Jared kicked out hard with one of his legs, striking something solid. He felt the grip that held him slip, and he pulled himself forward, yanking his backpack out of their grasp. The contents spilled out and Jared was barely able to snatch up the Guide in time. Reaching around in the grass, he picked up the stone and scrambled to where Mallory was. Then he brought the stone to his eye and looked.

"Six o'clock," he shouted, and Mallory whirled, striking in that direction, catching a goblin across the ear. It howled. Rapier blades didn't have points but they sure stung when they hit.

"Shorter, they're shorter." Jared managed to pull himself to his feet so that he was standing with his back against Mallory's. All five goblins were circling them.

One lunged from the right. "Three o'clock," Jared shouted.

Mallory knocked the goblin to the ground easily.

"Twelve o'clock! Nine o'clock! Seven o'clock!" They were rushing all at once, and Jared didn't think Mallory could possibly manage. He hefted the field guide and swung it as hard as he could at the nearest goblin.

Thwack! The book hit the goblin hard enough to send it sprawling backward.

All five goblins were circling them.

Mallory had knocked down two more with hard blows. Now they circled more warily, gnashing teeth of glass and stone.

There was a strange call, like a cross between a bark and a whistle.

At that sound, the goblins retreated one by one into the woods.

Jared collapsed onto the grass. His side hurt and he was out of breath.

"They're gone," Jared said. He held out the stone to Mallory. "Look."

Mallory sat down next to him and held it up to her eye. "I don't see anything, but I didn't see anything a minute ago either."

"They still might come back." Jared rolled over and opened the Guide, flipping through the pages quickly. "Read this."

"'Goblins travel in roving bands looking for trouble.'" Mallory scowled at the words.

Jared's gaze fell on the illustration of those horrible teeth.

Surely not. Surely there was some other explanation.

Mallory took a deep breath and pointed to the illustration. "It's going to be dark soon, and with eyes like that, they probably have better night vision than we do."

That was pretty smart. Jared resolved to write a note in the Guide about it when they got Simon back. He took off the eyepiece and slid the stone into place again, but the clamps were too loose to hold it.

"It doesn't work," Jared said.

"You have to adjust it," said Mallory. "We need a screwdriver or something."

Jared took a pocketknife from the back pocket of his pants. It had a screwdriver, a little knife, a magnifying glass, a file, bent scissors, and a place where there had once been a toothpick. Screwing down the clamps carefully, he fitted the stone into place.

"Here, let me tie it on your head right." Mallory knotted the leather straps until the monocle-apparatus was on tight. Jared had to squint a little to see properly, but it was

Time to find Simon

much better than before.

"Take this," Mallory said, and handed him a practice rapier. The end wasn't pointed, though, so he wasn't sure how much real damage it could do.

Still, it felt better to be armed. Tucking the Guide into his backpack, tightening the straps, and holding the sword in front of him, Jared started back down the hill into the darkening woods.

It was time to find Simon.

Find more adventure in

TROLL TROUBLE
and
GREAT ESCAPE

This episode has found its end,
but please don't close the book—
this chapter's new for those of you
who dare to take a look!

"The book. Give the book!"

Lost Chapter
GOBLINS ATTACK

IN WHICH Thimbletack Solves a Riddle and Becomes a Boggart

Thimbletack watched a whorl of dirt and hair blow across the floorboards into a patch of summer sunlight and rested his head on his hands with a heavy sigh. He didn't need to worry about people noticing him or the dust. There was no one to notice. There had been no one in the house for a long time.

Leaning back in his bent-wire chair, he remembered the day Lucinda left with her cousin, Melvina. Lucinda's black-and-silver hair was twisted in a bun and she carried a suitcase in each of her thin hands. Thimbletack had helped her pack them, folding each garment with starched precision.

"I'll be back from the hospital soon," Lucinda called.

Thimbletack's whiskers quivered, but he couldn't reply. Melvina would hear him.

"Who are you talking to?" Melvina wore a pantsuit and a necklace of large, white plastic beads that one of her hands seemed to constantly twist.

"No one," Lucinda said, shaking her head. "Just the house."

"See? Like I told you—you're alone too much," Melvina said. "Imagine! Talking to a house! A little supervised rest will do you good."

Almost twenty-five years had passed since then. During that time, Thimbletack had dusted and cleaned and polished. He made brooms sweep across the floor and rugs shake themselves like dogs. He wanted the place to be spotless for when Lucy came home. A brownie is supposed to keep the house clean and orderly, and he wanted to be a good brownie. He kept imagining her walking through the door and smiling at how well he'd kept up the place. If everything was perfect, maybe she'd stay this time.

One afternoon Thimbletack had stepped out on the lawn to mop the front steps when a sweaty, cold claw snatched him up so fast he forgot to scream.

A twisted face full of jagged glass teeth peered back at him. A goblin.

"Let me go!" Thimbletack shouted, squirming. "I'm no foe!"

The goblin shook its warty, froggy head. "The book. Give the book! Master wants the book!"

59

Thimbletack knew what book it wanted. Lucinda's father had made a field guide, cataloging not just the habits and habitats of faeries, but also their weaknesses and strengths. Thimbletack also knew how disastrous it would be for the book to fall into the hands of a creature intent on exploiting those weaknesses.

Quickly, other goblins came out of the bushes until ten of them surrounded him. One wore a scarf and another had a scar covering one eye, but most of them looked too similar to tell apart. Similar and terrifying. Thimbletack twisted in the glass-toothed goblin's grasp, then looked over at the mop. He could make it strike like a club without even touching it, but there were so many goblins that he wasn't sure if he could get them all.

"Like a little mousie," one of them said, smacking its lips, drool running down its chin like tears.

Thimbletack knew that Arthur Spiderwick had locked the book in an iron box. Iron burned faerie skin, so even if he told them where the book was, they probably couldn't get past the iron. But he didn't want their muddy feet tramping across his clean floors. And he was afraid. Even if they couldn't find a way to get into the box, their master, the ogre, might.

"What about a contest?" Thimbletack gasped as the fist that held him tightened. He thought about biting the rubbery fingers that held him, but he was afraid his teeth wouldn't even puncture the thick skin. "Try to best my test."

"How about he squashes you to pulp?" one of the goblins asked, and the others cackled.

"I'll ask you a riddle," Thimbletack said, "and if you answer right, I'll lead you to the book tonight. But you tell a riddle too, and if I'm correct, then you agree to let me go, direct?"

The goblins looked at each other dimly and grunted. Finally the one that held him nodded. "Ask your stupid riddle."

"You have to loosen your grip," the brownie said. "I can't breathe enough to quip."

"You breathe good enough to talk," said the goblin.

Thimbletack scowled. He resisted biting and offered his riddle. "What is fetched at night, but lost during the day, floats on the sea, but is never wet by spray?"

The goblins looked at one another. The one wearing a scarf scowled and said, "A boat?" But the other two shook their heads. "Maybe butter?" another suggested.

This was his chance! Thimbletack used his magic to make a stick strike the scarved goblin in the head. The scarved goblin turned toward the glass-toothed goblin that held Thimbletack and grunted. "Why'd you hit me?" he demanded, pale eyes narrowing.

"It wasn't me!" said the glass-toothed goblin.

"Was too!" The scarved goblin pushed him. Thimbletack used that moment to slip out of the glass-toothed goblin's hand and jump through the brass mail slot. He slid across the polished wood of the floor and heard the goblins scream with rage.

"I'll give you a boon," he yelled to them. "The answer's the moon!"

They gnashed their teeth and scrabbled at the mail slot.

Heart still pounding in his tiny chest, Thimbletack hopped up onto a cushioned chair to peer out one of the windows. He frowned. It wasn't fair that he had to protect the book after Arthur and Lucinda had left him all alone. He'd cared about them. He kept everything perfect for them. He'd been good and they'd left him anyway.

He was suddenly tired of protecting them and keeping the place clean for them. He was tired of looking out the window for a car that never came. He was tired of being a brownie.

He could feel himself swelling up with hate. His shoulders tightened as if anger was a heavy burden. His fingers clenched into claws. He could feel himself changing. If he didn't calm himself, he would become a boggart.

Magic roared up in him, hurling a bucket of soapy water across the room. He watched the liquid soak the carpet and trickle between the floorboards. He saw where water splashed the soot in the fireplace, spreading black filth.

He felt his face twist, and was dismayed to find himself smiling.